Every new generation of children is enthralled by the famous stories in our Well Loved Tales series. Younger ones love to have the story read to them. Older children will enjoy the exciting stories in an easy-to-read text.

British Library Cataloguing in Publication Data
Davies, Kath
    Peter and the wolf.—(Well loved tales; 606D).
    I. Title   II. Stevenson, Peter, 1953-
823'.914[J]
    ISBN 0-7214-1116-9

First edition

Published by Ladybird Books Ltd Loughborough Leicestershire UK
Ladybird Books Inc Auburn Maine 04210 USA

Printed in England

Peter and the Wolf

retold for easy reading
by KATH DAVIES

illustrated by PETER STEVENSON

Ladybird Books

Once upon a time there was a boy called
Peter, who lived with his grandfather in a little
house beside a green meadow.

Grandfather knew of all kinds of dangers in
the forest nearby and he tried to keep Peter
safe. One day he said, "You must never leave

the garden or go into the meadow alone, Peter.
The hungry wolf might come out of the forest
and eat you up.''

Peter did not answer. He loved animals and
birds, and he was sorry that the wolf was
hungry. He wasn't at all afraid of it.

Early one morning, Peter opened the garden gate, and went into the green meadow. He looked across the grass to the forest, but the wolf was nowhere to be seen. Peter walked on and on.

High up in the branches of a tree sat a small bird. When Peter was close to the tree, the bird said, "Hello, Peter! What are you doing here all alone?"

"Oh!" said Peter, looking up. "You made me jump! I'm just out for a walk. Have you seen the wolf today?"

"No," said the bird. "I haven't seen him, and what's more, I don't *want* to see him." He went on, "That wolf's always hungry, and when he's hungry, he will eat *anything*. Rabbits, chickens, lambs, ducks. *Anything*." He looked over Peter's shoulder. "There's a fine, fat duck," he said. "I'm sure the wolf would like to eat her. You'd better warn her about him."

Peter turned round to see a duck waddling up to him. She had followed him out through the garden gate because she wanted to swim in the pond in the meadow.

"Hello, Peter," she said. "It's a fine day for a swim. I'm glad you left the garden gate open."

"Oh dear!" said Peter. "I hope Grandfather

doesn't see it. He told me to stay in the
garden.''

Peter walked on towards the pond with the
duck, and the small bird watched them go.
When they came to the water's edge, the duck
shook out her feathers. She was ready to swim.

Peter said goodbye and went on by himself.

The small bird flew down to the pond.

"Hey, duck!" he said. "Why did you walk to the pond? It can't be easy to walk on such flat webbed feet. Why didn't you fly like me? What kind of a bird are you if you can't fly?"

The duck looked down at him.

"Fly?" she said. "Fly? Who wants to fly? I can fly if I want to, but I don't. I want to swim. And don't be rude about my feet, because webbed feet are made for swimming." She turned her back and dived into the pond.

"Come on in," she called. "The water's lovely!"

The small bird jumped back quickly from the edge of the pond. "Who, me?" he twittered. "Swim? You must be joking. I don't swim." He fluttered his feathers nervously.

"Aha!" said the duck. "You mean you *can't* swim? What kind of a bird are you, then?"

The small bird hopped up and down in rage, the duck swam round and round the pool, and the argument went on. They were so busy arguing that they did not hear Peter come back. He stood near the pond in the long grass, and he watched them. They were very funny.

Suddenly Peter saw the long grass swaying to and fro. A large striped cat was crawling through the grass towards the small bird. The cat was hungry and she was saying to herself, "That bird will never see me, he is much too busy shouting at the duck. I'll have him for dinner."

She came closer, crouching low in the grass. Her tail twitched. Just as she was ready to jump, Peter shouted, "The cat, the cat! Oh! Look out, bird!"

The cat sprang forward. She stretched her claws to catch the bird – and he flew straight up into the nearest tree.

She hissed and spat, as all cats do when they are angry.

Peter looked up at the small bird in the tree.

"Well," said Peter, "you are very lucky indeed. The cat almost had you for dinner!"

"I know," said the bird. "Thanks, Peter."

Then Peter spoke to the cat. She was still angry, and she lashed her tail from side to side.

"Cat," said Peter, "you should be ashamed of yourself. Go away and don't chase the bird again. If you are hungry, go into the garden. I will give you some food when I go home."

The cat did not reply. She stalked away in a huff, her tail held high. When she reached the long grass, she sat down and began to wash herself. "See if I care," she thought. "Next time, I'll get that bird."

Not far away, Peter laughed, the bird sang and the duck quacked. They made a great deal of noise in the meadow, because they were so happy.

After a while, Grandfather came out into the garden and saw that the garden gate was open. There was no sign of Peter. Grandfather was worried because he knew that Peter might be in danger. Then he heard the happy noises in the meadow, and he looked over the garden wall. He saw Peter, the duck and the small bird, and he was very angry.

"Peter!" he called. "Come here at once." Then he went out into the field to fetch Peter.

Peter heard his grandfather shouting. He stopped laughing, and ran towards him. "Come with me!" Grandfather ordered, and marched Peter back to the garden. He locked the garden gate behind them.

Grandfather turned to Peter and said, "How many times have I told you not to leave the garden? You know the hungry wolf might come out of the forest. Do you want him to eat you for his dinner?"

Peter said nothing.

"Well?" said Grandfather. "Did you hear what I said?"

"Yes," muttered Peter. He was sorry that he had disobeyed, but he still thought that Grandfather was making too much fuss.

Grandfather went into the house, and took the key with him because he did not trust Peter to stay in the garden.

Peter was bored and unhappy as he wandered round the garden. The small bird tried to help. He flew to a tree near the garden wall and sang to Peter. But it was no good. Peter didn't cheer up.

Meanwhile, the huge hungry wolf *did* come out of the forest, and terrified everyone. The small bird saw him first, and called in alarm to warn the duck.

The cat heard the bird's warning as well. She hissed in fright and climbed straight up the tree.

The duck quacked loudly. She was so frightened that she jumped right out of the pond. The wolf was coming – and he was the biggest wolf that she had ever seen.

The wolf saw the duck jump out of the
pond, and he ran after her. She ran as fast as
she could, but the wolf ran faster.

In a moment he caught her. He opened his
mouth – and swallowed her in one gulp. She
was gone. A feather or two on the grass was all
that was left of the duck.

The small bird and the cat sat high up in the tree together, looking down at the wolf. The bird had forgotten to be afraid of the cat. And the cat had forgotten that her own dinner was sitting beside her in the same tree.

The wolf was very pleased with the fine dinner he had caught! He wished he had not swallowed it all at once though. His mother was always telling him not to eat so quickly.

He sat looking up at the bird and the cat, and he thought, "Ho, hum, do I see more dinner?"

Then he began to prowl round the tree.
Above him, the small bird and the cat were too
frightened to move.

Peter had seen what had happened. "Silly,
silly duck," he sighed. "She would have been
safe if she'd stayed in the pond."

Then he had an idea. He knew how he could
save the cat and the bird, and he wasn't afraid
of the wolf.

Peter found a long rope and ran out into the garden with it, straight to the garden wall. He tied the rope carefully around his waist, then he climbed up the wall. He scratched his hands and scraped his knees, but he did not mind.

As soon as Peter was sitting safely on top of the wall, he untied the rope from his waist and began to make a loop in one end of it.

From his high seat, Peter could see down into the meadow. He could see the wolf – and he could hear him growling. Peter could see the small bird and the cat sitting in the tree as well. The cat's tail was beating against the tree branch, but the bird was absolutely still. Peter knew that they were both very frightened.

The wolf was still prowling around the tree. Round and round he went. Sometimes he stopped to rest, and then he looked up at the cat and the bird in the branches above him. He growled horribly. The cat and the bird thought that he was growling at them, but he wasn't.

He was beginning to feel quite ill. Inside him
the duck was still alive and she was kicking his
stomach hard. She was very cross, and she
thought that if she could make the wolf hiccup,
she might be able to jump out.

The wolf felt worse and worse.

Peter called out to the bird, "Fly round the wolf's head. Make him look at you. Then he won't see what I am doing." The wolf was growling so loudly he couldn't hear what Peter was saying.

So the bird flew round the wolf's head. The wolf snapped at him, but he kept on flying round. Soon the wolf felt quite dizzy. As the cat watched, she thought how brave the bird was, and she was glad after all that she hadn't eaten him for her dinner.

Peter finished making the loop at the end of the rope. He tied one end of the rope to the tree, and he let the other end down carefully over the wolf.

By now the wolf was feeling very ill indeed, and he did not see Peter above him with the rope. Then suddenly, something pulled his tail very hard. It was Peter's rope! Now the wolf couldn't run away. The more he tried, the tighter the rope became round his tail.

All at once there was a noise in the forest.
There were shouts and cries, and bangs and
crashes. People were riding through the trees
and bushes, firing guns as they came. They
were hunting the wolf.

When the hunters rode out of the forest into the meadow, they saw the wolf beneath the tree, and they fired their guns to frighten him.

Peter shouted, "Don't shoot! Ride over here. We've caught the wolf and he can't get away."

The hunters rode up to the tree. They looked down at the wolf held fast at the end of Peter's rope. Then they looked up at Peter, the bird and the cat, and they were astonished.

"How did you manage to catch the wolf?" they asked Peter. So he told them what had happened. The hunters looked at the wolf, who was now lying down with his eyes closed.

"What are you going to do with him?" they asked. "He doesn't look terribly fierce." The wolf opened his eyes and groaned.

"I don't think he's feeling very well," said
Peter. "We're going to take him to the zoo.
The zoo keepers will look after him, and he
won't be able to catch any more of my friends
and eat them for his dinner."

The hunters asked Peter who the wolf had
eaten for dinner, and Peter told them about the
duck. "Poor duck," said the hunters.

Just then Grandfather came out into the garden and saw Peter on top of the garden wall. "What's going on now?" he called. "What are you doing on the wall?"

Then he saw the hunters and the wolf, and his face turned pale. When he went nearer, he saw that Peter was holding the rope, and the rope was holding the wolf. At that moment, Grandfather's face grew red with rage.

Before he could say one word, the hunters told him how Peter had caught the wolf. Now Grandfather didn't know whether to be proud of Peter or to be angry with him. He glared at his grandson, but there was a twinkle in his eye.

So they all set off for the zoo, with Peter leading the procession. After him came the hunters with the wolf. The wolf was feeling better, because the duck was having a rest. She had stopped kicking inside his stomach. Grandfather followed the wolf, and the cat walked beside him. The small bird went with them.

The hunters blew their hunting horns, and everyone came out to see the wolf. They laughed and cheered, then they ran to tell their friends all about it.

The cat and the bird were happy because the wolf was going away. The hunters were happy because Peter had caught the wolf. Grandfather was happy because Peter was safe. Even the wolf was glad that he was going to a fine new home. He hoped the keepers would take away the pain in his stomach.

The duck was not too happy inside the wolf, but she knew that the zoo keepers would soon rescue her. She quacked and quacked. All the people who heard her were puzzled, and kept looking around them. Wherever could she be?

As for Peter, he was very happy indeed, because he knew that the wolf was never going to be hungry again.